A Sweet New Year for Ren

Written by
Michelle Sterling

Illustrations by
Dung Ho

A Paula Wiseman Book
Simon & Schuster Books for Young Readers
New York London Toronto Sydney New Delhi

A Note from the Author

Growing up, I loved hearing my father tell stories about his childhood in the Philippines, and to this day, I still do. *A Sweet New Year for Ren* was inspired by our Chinese heritage, by stories of my dad celebrating Lunar New Year as a boy, and by my family's love for traditions and beautiful times spent together throughout the years.

Lunar New Year is a time for extended family to gather together to celebrate and usher in the new year. Red decorations are hung all around because the color red is known as a very lucky color. Children pay their respects to elders and are given hong bao, or red envelopes, filled with crisp new bills.

Pineapples symbolize good fortune and prosperity in Chinese and Taiwanese cultures. Pineapple cakes originated in Taiwan and are often given as gifts wherever Lunar New Year is celebrated. In Singapore, Malaysia, and Indonesia, pineapple tarts are also baked and enjoyed during Lunar New Year. My hope is that readers will enjoy making this special dessert with their families at home!

—*Michelle Sterling*

SIMON & SCHUSTER BOOKS FOR YOUNG READERS • An imprint of Simon & Schuster Children's Publishing Division • 1230 Avenue of the Americas, New York, New York 10020 • Text © 2022 by Michelle Sterling • Illustration © 2022 by Dung Ho • Book design by Sarah Creech © 2022 by Simon & Schuster, Inc. • All rights reserved, including the right of reproduction in whole or in part in any form. • SIMON & SCHUSTER BOOKS FOR YOUNG READERS and related marks are trademarks of Simon & Schuster, Inc. • For information about special discounts for bulk purchases, please contact Simon & Schuster Special Sales at 1-866-506-1949 or business@simonandschuster.com. • The Simon & Schuster Speakers Bureau can bring authors to your live event. For more information or to book an event, contact the Simon & Schuster Speakers Bureau at 1-866-248-3049 or visit our website at www.simonspeakers.com. • The text for this book was set in Iowan Old Style. • The illustrations for this book were rendered in Photoshop. • Manufactured in Thailand • 0722 SCP • First Edition • 2 4 6 8 10 9 7 5 3 1 • Library of Congress Cataloging-in-Publication Data • Names: Sterling, Michelle, author. | Ho, Dung, illustrator. • Title: A sweet new year for Ren / Michelle Sterling ; illustrated by Dung Ho. • Description: New York : Simon & Schuster Books for Young Readers, [2022] | "A Paula Wiseman Book." | Audience: Ages 4-8. | Audience: Grades 2-3. | Summary: Ren has always been too little to help make her favorite pineapple cakes for the Lunar New Year, but when her one-of-a-kind brother Charlie arrives for the festivities, with his help, she finally gets her chance. Includes recipe for pineapple cakes. • Identifiers: LCCN 2021047310 (print) | LCCN 2021047311 (ebook) | ISBN 9781534496606 (hardcover) | ISBN 9781534496613 (ebook) • Subjects: CYAC: Chinese New Year—Fiction. | Baking—Fiction. | Chinese Americans—Fiction. | LCGFT: Picture books. • Classification: LCC PZ7.1.S74433 Sw 2022 (print) | LCC PZ7.1.S74433 (ebook) | DDC [E]—dc23 • LC record available at https://lccn.loc.gov/2021047310 • LC ebook record available at https://lccn.loc.gov/2021047311

For my father
—M.S.

For Phuong Dung,
my little sister
—D.H.

My eyes open wide on an early morning.
It smells like Lunar New Year is almost here!

Every year I sit and watch
    everyone crowded around the butcher block,
    hoping and hoping that I will get to help make pineapple cakes.
        "You're still too little, Ren," Mama always says.

But I've grown one whole inch since last Lunar New Year.
    No, two inches!
        Will I get to help, finally?

Bright oranges, tangerines, and
pomelos bounce together into a bowl
    sprinkled with kumquats,
        shiny and tiny.

"Can I help, Baba?" I ask.
"I'm afraid you're still too little, Ren."

Out we scramble
to find our final ingredients
        for tomorrow's feast.

A fresh silver sea bass is Baba's favorite,
with splashes of soy and slivers of scallions.
        I poke the fish's glassy scales as it slips
            and squeaks into a bag.

Bright green garlic chives
and sharp, spicy ginger
     for Mama's famous dumplings.
One day she'll pass on her recipe to me!
And I will keep it a secret, of course.

One pleat after another,
Mama's expert fingers fold dumplings in a whir.
   She and Uncle Jian race to see who can fold the fastest,
      like they did when they were kids.

                              Rows and rows of dumplings
                                 fill up our table.
                              Mixing, rolling, filling, folding.

Cooking in a foggy steam.
Watching and waiting, I smell that they're done.
"Can I help?"
"You're still too little, Ren.
We're in a big hurry!"

Bubbling in hot water
   are the longest noodles Auntie Weili could find
      to eat for a long, long life.
         She's careful not to break
            the endless strands.

"Can I help stir?"
"You're still too little, Ren.
  It's too hot!" Auntie Weili says.

"Xin nian kuai le, everyone!"
Charlie is back!

Charlie, who would always bring me taro milk tea
    when he picked me up from Sunday violin lessons.
Charlie, who always had a wide pot of congee simmering on the stove
    the nights Mama and Baba had to work late.
Charlie, my one-of-a-kind brother!

I want to show Charlie that I'm a good cook.
But the pineapples keep pricking my fingers.

Plop! The butter slips out of the wrapper
onto our sticky linoleum floor.
Clouds of flour fly into the air.

Laughing, he cleans up the mess with me.
Mashing butter and flour together,

Charlie shows me how to roll out the dough.
Not too thick, not too thin.
Together we make it just right.
"That's it, Mei-Mei!"

"I know that delicious smell!" Auntie Amy exclaims.

"Ren, be gentle when you push the dough into the molds!"

"Look, Mama!"

"Ren, you're finally old enough to help make pineapple cakes!" Mama beams.

Happy pineapple cakes baking.
Their golden crust and rich pineapple jam
smelling like butter
and sweet time together.

"I'm hungry," says Jules.

"I'm hungrier!" Marnie pipes up.

"No one will notice if we take one . . .

or three!"

Our tray of togetherness, crowded with
candied lotus root and winter melon,
for Auntie Amy and Uncle Jian.
Dried kumquats for Charlie,
lively and tart.

My twin cousins, Jules and Marnie, gulp down
one sugary coconut slice after another.
A handful of lucky red candy for me!
So many wishes for a sweet year.

Red envelopes for everyone!
 The sky glowing red with lanterns,
firecrackers dancing, snapping, cracking.

My favorite part of the new year.
Everyone is here, together.

Pineapple cakes are for eating,
sharing,
celebrating,
and starting this sweet new year
with each other,
thankful for each other.

Our stomachs are full and happy,
like our hearts.

Pineapple Cakes

MAKES 25 CAKES

Please do not attempt without adult supervision

FILLING

2 20-ounce/567 g cans of crushed pineapple in juice
1 ½ cups/355 ml water
1 cup/200 g sugar
1 tbsp/15 g unsalted butter

TOOLS NEEDED

10 square aluminum pineapple cake molds
(4.8 cm x 4.8 cm x 1.8 cm) with a matching press

CRUST

1 ¾ cups/210 g all-purpose flour
2 tbsp/15 g cornstarch
¼ cup/25 g dry milk
½ tsp salt
2 sticks/1 cup/226 g unsalted butter, softened
3 tbsp/45 g cream cheese, softened
½ cup/55 g powdered sugar, sifted
1 egg yolk
2 tbsp/35 g sweetened condensed milk
1/2 tsp vanilla
extra flour for shaping

MAKE THE FILLING

1. Drain the pineapple in a fine mesh sieve placed over a large mixing bowl. Do not press or squeeze any juice from the pulp.
2. Place the pulp, water, and sugar into a large, non-stick pan over high heat. Mix the ingredients together. Bring the pulp to a boil, then lower the heat to a simmer. Continue to simmer for about 1 hour. Stir occasionally.
3. When all the extra liquid has evaporated, you will start to hear the pulp sizzle. Add the butter and lower the heat. Continue to cook the pineapple for about 30 minutes. Stir and flip the pulp frequently so that the pulp doesn't burn. When the pineapple filling is done, it will look like a slightly glossy, very thick jam that is able to hold shape.
4. Transfer the filling to a bowl, then cover and cool completely. Measure out 25 2-teaspoon/18-g portions, then roll each portion into a ball. Place the balls in an airtight container. Set aside in the fridge.

MAKE THE CRUST

1. Sift together the flour, cornstarch, dry milk, and salt. Set aside.
2. In a large mixing bowl, cream the butter and cream cheese together. For best results, mix by hand using a rubber spatula.
3. Cream the powdered sugar in with the butter mixture. Mix in the egg yolk, condensed milk, and vanilla until everything is combined.
4. Add the sifted flour blend to the butter mixture and mix until everything is just combined. Scrape the bottom and sides of the bowl. Do not overmix.
5. Wrap the dough in a large piece of plastic wrap and shape it into a flat round. Place into the fridge to chill for at least 1 hour.

SHAPE THE CAKES

1. Remove the dough from the fridge. Measure out 25 2-tablespoon/25 g portions, then roll each portion into a ball. Set aside.
2. Preheat the oven to 350° F. Place 10 square pineapple cake metal molds 1 inch apart on a large baking sheet fitted with a silicone baking mat or parchment paper.
3. Remove the pineapple filling balls from the fridge. Have a bowl of bench flour set aside for shaping.
4. Roll a dough ball into the bowl of flour. Dust off any excess. With lightly floured hands, flatten a ball, then roll in flour and dust off any excess.
5. Place the ball inside a metal mold. Lightly dust the flat press with bench flour. Use the press to compact the filled dough ball into the mold. Repeat this process to make more cakes.
6. Bake the cakes in their metal molds for 12 minutes on one side, then remove the baking sheet from the oven. Using tongs and a cookie spatula, carefully flip each cake over, metal mold intact. Bake for an additional 5 to 7 minutes until golden brown.
7. Remove the cakes from the oven. Use tongs to remove the metal molds. Use a spatula to transfer the cakes to a cooling rack.
8. Pineapple cakes taste wonderful fresh out of the oven, but are even more delicious the day after baking. To store, place the cooled cakes in an airtight container and eat within 7 days.
9. Enjoy!

TIPS

- Pineapple cakes are commonly enjoyed as squares, but they can also be shaped as rectangles, rounds, or even tarts. However you choose to shape them, you'll want to keep the volume ratio of filling to dough at roughly 1:3 to create the perfect bite.
- If you don't have any metal molds, no problem! Shape the cakes as flattened rounds, baking them seam side down. Bake them for 15 minutes. No need to flip!
- To use fresh pineapple, simply substitute 3 cups/670 g of grated fresh pineapple pulp for the canned pineapple pulp. Remove the top, base, skin, and core from 2 pineapples. Use a coarse grater and drain the pineapple over a fine mesh sieve before measuring it.

REFERENCES FOR MORE LUNAR NEW YEAR RECIPES
Chinese Soul Food: A Friendly Guide for Homemade Dumplings, Stir-Fries, Soups, and More by Hsiao-Ching Chou (Sasquatch Books, 2018)
The Breath of a Wok by Grace Young and Alan Richardson (Simon & Schuster, 2004)
The Wisdom of the Chinese Kitchen: Classic Family Recipes for Celebration and Healing by Grace Young (Simon & Schuster Editions, 1999)
Chinese Heritage Cooking from My American Kitchen by Shirley Chung (Page Street Publishing Co., 2018)
At the Chinese Table by Carolyn Phillips (W. W. Norton & Company, 2021)
All Under Heaven by Carolyn Phillips (Ten Speed Press, 2016)
The Food of Taiwan: Recipes from the Beautiful Island by Cathy Erway (Houghton Mifflin Harcourt, 2015)

Recipe © Bonnie Eng, food writer